S0-BSW-940

Silly Sally

by Audrey Wood

SCHOLASTIC INC.

New York   Toronto   London   Auckland   Sydney

No part of this publication may be reproduced in whole or in part, or stored in a retrieval system, or transmitted in any form or by any means, electronic, mechanical, photocopying, recording, or otherwise, without written permission of the publisher. For information regarding permission, write to Permissions Department. Harcourt Brace and Company, 8th Floor, Orlando, FL 32887.

ISBN 0-590-22562-6

Copyright © 1992 by Audrey Wood. All rights reserved. Published by Scholastic Inc., 555 Broadway, New York, NY 10012, by arrangement with Harcourt Brace and Company.

48 47 46 45 44   8 9/0

Printed in the U.S.A.   08

First Scholastic printing, February 1995

The paintings in this book were done in Winsor & Newton watercolors on Arches watercolor paper.
The display type was hand lettered by the illustrator, based on a rendering by Brenda Walton, Sacramento, California.

For Ann and Warren Wallerstein

Silly Sally went to town,
walking backwards, upside down.

On the way she met a pig,
a silly pig,

they danced a jig.

Silly Sally went to town,
dancing backwards, upside down.

On the way she met a dog,
a silly dog,

they played leapfrog.

Silly Sally went to town,
leaping backwards, upside down.

On the way she met a loon,
a silly loon,

they sang a tune.

Silly Sally went to town,
singing backwards, upside down.

On the way she met a sheep,
a silly sheep,

they fell asleep.

Now how did Sally get to town,
sleeping backwards, upside down?

Along came Neddy Buttercup,
walking forwards, right side up.

He tickled the pig
who danced a jig.

He tickled the dog
who played leapfrog.

He tickled the loon
who sang a tune.

He tickled the sheep
who fell asleep.

He tickled Sally,
who woke right up.

She tickled Neddy Buttercup.

And that's how Sally got to town,

walking backwards, upside down.